The Programmed Pastor

The Programmed Pastor

R. J. MATHIEU

RESOURCE *Publications* · Eugene, Oregon

THE PROGRAMMED PASTOR

Resource Publications
An Imprint of Wipf and Stock Publishers
199 W. 8th Ave., Suite 3
Eugene, OR 97401

www.wipfandstock.com

PAPERBACK ISBN: 979-8-3852-2735-8
HARDCOVER ISBN: 979-8-3852-2736-5
EBOOK ISBN: 979-8-3852-2737-2

VERSION NUMBER 10/17/24

Contents

Chapter 1

The Board Meeting

Introducing the Actually Authentic Android
Equipped with trillions of terabytes of storage
Virtually Indestructible
Customizable: Choose your robot's gender, race, height, hair color,
eye color, and more!
Able to be programmed for endless tasks and social situations.
So convincing no one will ever know it's not human.
Don't wait!
Get your Actually Authentic Android today for the low, low price of
$999.99 plus $59.99 shipping and handling.
$199.99 extra for 2-day rush shipping.
Log in to our easy-to-use website:
www.humanprogramming.com
And create the Actually Authentic Android of your dreams!

As HUBERT LOOKED UP from reading the ad in his electronic newspaper every member of the church board gazed at their treasurer with looks that were a mix of amusement and shock. Dottie pretended to become more interested in her coffee which was black and cold and could not possibly be less interesting. She was actually secretly reading about a new television show on her phone. Mark, who was leading the meeting, took a bite of his brownie before breaking the silence.

"Well, Hubert. That is a mighty interesting ad, but I don't see what it's got to do with our dilemma of finding a new pastor for our church."

Hubert looked nervous for a minute, but then forced a smile.

"Well, I've been thinking. It's been a rough last several years. In five years, we've gone through three pastors and no interim pastor has lasted more than a month. The last one didn't even make it through his first and only sermon. He had a heart attack and was pronounced dead at the scene. The congregation hasn't liked any of our suggestions for pastoral candidates. What if we bought one of these Actually Authentic Androids and created it to be all the things that the congregation has told us they want their pastor to be?"

Most of the board members gasped, but Bob stuffed a big wad of brownie into his mouth.

"Are you crazy, Hubert?" asked Maddie, sounding noticeably condescending. "I thought you quit smoking pot years ago."

"I did," answered Hubert, sheepishly. "But what else are we going to do? It doesn't seem like anything makes our congregation happy."

"Does that really matter?" continued Maddie, sounding completely uninterested. "I think we're wasting our time trying to make them happy. It can't be done."

Across from Hubert sat Sandy, the oldest board member. She was the one who ran the church during the week, but with also running her own online business and the constant complaining from the congregation, she was finding this task increasingly taxing.

"Yes. I quite agree the congregation is a lost cause," said Sandy, somewhat sullenly. "On the other hand, a machine might be an ideal choice to pastor this congregation. A machine won't care if the congregation complains. It hasn't got any feelings."

"Ah, yes. An android will always act in the most logical manner," reasoned Mary. "It won't cave under pressure."

Bob stuffed another big wad of brownie into his mouth.

"I am beginning to see certain advantages of having an android as a pastor," Mark mused. "But could we program the android to fulfill all the duties of a pastor?"

"How could we?" inquired Buford. "Androids aren't capable of making moral judgments, something a pastor must be able to do."

"Ah, but I think Mary already made an astute observation," said Hubert. "An android will always act in the most logical manner. Evil is never logical. Therefore, the android will always do what is good and it will insist on others doing good."

"Who would have thought that it would be the android which lacks a moral compass that would most easily live and promote the Christian life?" Mark marveled.

"Perhaps humanity would be better off if God had made us all robots," Sandy spouted.

Hubert beamed.

"Well, I think we've all come to a decision."

"But perhaps we ought to reconsider," suggested Maddie. "After all, Buford brought up a good point. The plan does have certain risks. We ought to be wary."

Hubert cast a glance directly at Bob. Bob stuffed another big wad of brownie into his mouth.

"All those in favor of making an Actually Authentic Android our pastor raise your hand now," Mark motivated.

Everyone but Buford and Maddie raised their hands.

"Meeting adjourned," Mark moved.

But Bob had already made a beeline to the toilet. His stomach hurt like hell.

Chapter 2

The New Pastor

THE CHURCH BOARD SAT down in their seats, all of them staring at the huge box in the center of the room. The Actually Authentic Android had arrived just a couple of days ago. Sandy had alerted the other board members of its arrival and Hubert, Mark, and Bob had helped haul the big box into the church. Excited as most of the board members were about the arrival of their new pastor, none of them had yet opened the box. Pastor Matthew Love still stood shut up and silent in his rectangular prison. All of the board members had gathered today to finally let him out and turn him on.

Buford and Maddie were still uneager about the Actually Authentic Android. Neither of them dared to approach the box. But with Hubert there was no hesitation. In a matter of minutes, he had the box open. Then Mark and Bob approached and helped Hubert take Pastor Matthew Love from his box.

Pastor Matthew Love was a beautiful robot with curly brown hair, a well-formed face and physique, and green eyes which would have gleamed like gold if they had been open at that moment. All of the board members gathered around their new pastor, although Maddie and Buford kept their distance.

Hubert seemed to be the most impressed among them. He ran his hand over the pastor's face briefly and then smiled.

"It's true. His skin looks and feels like the real thing," he said. "And look at his sharp threads. Baby blue dress shirt, black tie, black pants, and fine black leather shoes. Just turn him on, give him the good book, and he'll make a real fine pastor."

"Well, what are we waiting for?" asked Mark. "Let's turn him on. We've only a couple days before Sunday. We've got to get him ready."

"Yes. But the congregation will expect him to preach on Sunday," said Buford, looking baffled. "Is he going to be able to do that?"

"Sure. No problem," answered Hubert in an easygoing tone. "Sandy, Mark, and I spent a whole day customizing and programming him. We programmed him to do all the duties of a pastor, including preaching. He's got all kinds of Bibles downloaded into his storage. He has his own Wi-Fi receiver and we've got him hooked up to the church and parsonage Wi-Fi already. If he wants to he can even find some other pastor's sermon online and preach it."

"You're going to let the Actually Authentic Android live in the parsonage all by itself, and unattended?" asked Maddie, becoming bewildered.

"Of course," answered Mark. "Hubert and Sandy and I agreed that we should treat the robot like we would any pastor."

"And shouldn't we treat the robot as a person since he looks like one?" persisted Hubert. "Mark and Sandy and I feel very strongly that he should have his freedom and that we should pay him. He's our pastor after all, not our slave or property."

"Well, I certainly agree that we should treat the android kindly," said Maddie. "I only meant. . ."

"Good," interrupted Mark. "Glad to see that we are on the same page. Now how do we turn on the pastor, Hubert?"

Hubert knelt down and picked up the owner's manual off the floor of the big box. It was as thick as a graphic novel. He quickly flipped through the first couple of pages.

"Well, there's an on and off switch on the back of his head, hiding under his hair. It also says that it takes a minute or two for him to boot up. Once he does, his eyes will open, and he should start talking to us."

"And we expect this thing to run our church," blurted Buford, indignantly. "It's just some damn computer."

"Of course, he can," reiterated Mark. "We programmed him. Go ahead. Turn him on, Hubert."

Hubert went behind the Actually Authentic Android and pressed the button on the back of his head. Immediately, a soft sound like a cat purring began issuing forth from Pastor Matthew Love. Slowly his soft sea-green eyes opened and gazed kindly at the church board. Another moment passed and then the relaxing purring sound ceased and for the first time Pastor Matthew Love opened his mouth.

"Hello. I'm Pastor Matthew Love and I'm here to tell you that Jesus loves you," he said in a calm voice that sounded completely human with no hint of a robotic quality at all.

"Ah. You see that!" exclaimed Hubert. "He's perfect. The congregation will be delighted with him."

"I'm not so sure," Maddie began whispering to Mark. "And don't you think the congregation will want to know that he's a robot? I mean we used money that they tithed to the church to pay for this contraption."

"What does it matter?" Mark began whispering back to Maddie. "And why would it matter as long as they have the pastor they want? Now come on, Maddie. Introduce yourself. Let's make friends with the new pastor?"

Maddie shyly walked over to the robot and extended her hand to it. Shaking his hand, she said:

"Hello Pastor Matthew Love. My name is Madeline Madison. But everyone calls me Maddie. I am a member of the church board and the children's director as well."

"Nice to meet you, Maddie," replied Pastor Matthew Love, curving his mouth into a pleasant smile.

Then one by one each board member approached the pastor and introduced himself or herself, all except for Bob who shoved a piece of candy in his mouth, walked up to the android, waved shyly at him, and immediately wandered off.

"That is Bob," explained Mark, coming up after Bob to greet the pastor. "He's also on the board."

◆ ◆ ◆

And here's where you'll live."

Hubert opened the front door to the parsonage and stepped in, followed by Pastor Matthew Love, and then the others. The parsonage was a white building with red trim and a red door in the front and in the rear. The inside walls were all red except for the tile in the bathroom. This tile as well as the floors in the bathroom and in the kitchen was blue. Every other floor was covered in red carpet as thick as wool.

There was a dark green arm chair and sofa in the living room. A long coffee table stood a few feet in front of the sofa and an enormous flat-screen television stood a few feet in front of the long coffee table upon a strong stand. There were three bedrooms in the parsonage. Each one had a bed with red blankets and a red comfy chair that stood in front of a white desk. Each one also included a small closet. The kitchen had an electric stove and refrigerator, which were both white, and a red table and four red comfy chairs, one standing on each side of it. The kitchen was equipped with much counter and storage space which was all white.

Between two of the bedrooms was another closet, bigger than those in the bedrooms. This closet contained a vacuum cleaner, a variety of tools, and some other items for cleaning. As Hubert showed him around, Pastor Matthew Love looked all over, but there was no indication that he was impressed or felt anything at all.

"You can choose which bedroom you wish to use. Today is Friday, so you will have a couple of days to rest. On Sunday the service starts at 10 a.m. At 9 a.m., we will have donuts and coffee in the fellowship hall. We would like you to be in the fellowship hall at least a few minutes before then. You will also need to be ready to run the church service, including preaching the sermon. Are you good with that pastor?"

"Yes. It's no trouble. I'm Pastor Matthew Love and I'm here to tell people that Jesus loves them," replied the robot, his eyes emotionlessly fixed on Hubert the whole time.

"Wonderful," said Hubert ecstatically. "Well, you'll find plenty of food in the kitchen. And here are the keys to the parsonage and the church. And here is your first paycheck. We'll all see you on Sunday"

"Yes. Thank you," replied the robot as he took the things from Hubert's hands.

"Bye Pastor Matthew Love," said Hubert with a wave.

When all of the board had said good-bye to the android, except for Bob, who only waved, they exited the parsonage. Buford was the last to leave. He gazed at the pastor one last time before he pulled the parsonage door shut behind him.

◆ ◆ ◆

"This is a bad idea," said Buford when they had gone some ways from the parsonage. "Who knows what that android will do. We should have made it write a sermon and turned it off until Sunday morning."

All of the other board members except for Maddie looked shocked.

"I thought we agreed not to treat him like a slave," said Mark. "And anyway, he'll be quite alright. Besides all of the pastoral responsibilities we programmed him to handle the normal responsibilities of an adult. He can clean, cook, balance a budget, drive, you name it."

"Is it legal for that thing to drive?" asked Buford incredulously.

"Oh yes," answered Mark. "He comes with a fully legal driver's license and we upgraded him for international travel, so he also has a legal passport. We downloaded a map of our town and the surrounding towns into his memory and he comes equipped with the most advanced GPS on the market, so if he does leave the parsonage he won't get lost. Of course, he doesn't have a car yet, but he can buy one later if he wants."

"If he wants?" asked Maddie. "Does he have wants beyond what he was programmed to want?"

"Well. . ." began Mark with a nervous smile.

Maddie looked at Mark, Hubert, and Sandy harshly. There was notable anger in her voice.

"This is dangerous, you three. You have no idea what you've done."

She walked toward her beat-up, old car without another word. Buford likewise left without further conversation. Mary had an anxious look on her face, but said nothing. Dottie said good-bye and sauntered off toward her truck. Bob took a mint out of his pocket and stuck it in his mouth before walking off silently. Mark and Sandy looked crestfallen, but a smile broke over Hubert's face.

"Not to worry," he said, sounding genuinely happy. "Maddie and Buford have always been worriers. That android pastor is going to work out just fine."

Still smiling, Hubert strutted off toward his vehicle, a fancy green sports car. Both Mark and Sandy took one last look at the parsonage. Everything seemed quiet. Rain started to fall lightly from the sky and the two of them made for their vehicles.

Chapter 3

Meeting the Congregation

ON SUNDAY RAIN WAS still a reality, but it fell not much harder than when the church board left on Friday. The congregation had begun to file into the fellowship hall promptly at fifteen minutes past nine except for a few more faithful folks who had arrived around 8:45 a.m. Pastor Matthew Love himself was just arriving and he greeted the congregants with a smile and a handshake, introducing himself. At fifteen till ten he walked into the church sanctuary.

A small number of congregants trickled into the church at fifteen till ten. At ten after ten two big families with very noisy children walked into the sanctuary almost drowning out the hymn being sung. Maddie was reasonably irate at the parents, but said nothing. Ordinarily, these children would be in the children's church with her and nineteen-year-old Benjamin Cane in the small chapel, but since they were all to meet the possible new pastor, there was no children's church today.

It took about twelve minutes for all the children to settle down. Finally, it was time for the sermon. Pastor Matthew Love stood up in the pulpit and glanced around at the congregation. He was very nicely dressed and all the congregation seemed to anticipate his speaking. Even the children were becoming silent.

"I'm Pastor Matthew Love," said the Actually Authentic Android. "And I'm here to tell you that Jesus loves you."

The sanctuary roared with applause. Pastor Matthew Love went on.

"Jesus died on the cross for you. Jesus loves you madly. Jesus rose from the dead and if you will only believe in him he will give you eternal life. All it takes is belief. No matter what you have done Jesus loves you and accepts you. Do you want to be assured love, acceptance, and eternal life? Believe and you will be saved. Every sin you have ever committed and ever will commit will be wiped out for good. Nothing and nobody will be able to separate you from Jesus or his love. And once you ask Jesus into your heart you are saved once and for all. Nothing will ever change that. Dear beloved ones, I implore you to ask Jesus into your heart today if you have never done so. Don't miss out on Jesus's love and acceptance or on eternal life in heaven with him where there is no pain, no despair, and no death. Now who would like to accept Jesus into their heart today?"

Half of the room raised their hands. It had been such a long time since anyone in this church had accepted Jesus Christ into their heart. The Actually Authentic Android did not smile. He gazed at the congregation in a manner that suggested seriousness.

"Those of you who would like to receive Jesus into your heart repeat after me: I confess that I am a sinner and that Jesus died on the cross to save me from my sins and that he rose from the dead on the third day so that I might have eternal life. Today I ask Jesus to come into my life and to be the Savior of my life. Amen."

All the new converts repeated after the robot pastor. The rest of the congregation remained silent, including Hubert whose blank stare seemed to suggest that his consciousness was wandering about upon a sea of senseless oblique tranquility. Even the infants in the assembly did not stir, but lay asleep against the bosoms of their mothers.

When the prayer ended Pastor Matthew Love curved his mouth upwards mechanically. Hubert began to clap and nearly everyone in the crowd joined him. The Actually Authentic Android sat down quietly in his seat. The small worship band led the congregation in the closing song: "There's Nobody Happier Than Jesus and I am Happy with Him."

As soon as the song ended the whole assembly arose from their soft, cushioned maroon chairs. An older gentleman who had sat up in the front row came and shook hands with Pastor Matthew Love.

"That was the best sermon we've heard at this church in a long time and it was nice and short. You've certainly got my vote Pastor Matthew Love."

"Thank you," replied the pastor, smiling blandly.

Then the same older man blurted out loudly:

"Well, there really isn't any reason to vote now is there? I think we're all agreed with what ought to be done."

Every adult applauded, except for Maddie and Buford. Hubert's face filled with euphoria. Maddie learned over to Buford who stood next to her: "Well, it appears that they have at last found their pastor, programmed to their liking."

Chapter 4

A New Leader for the Board

IT WAS THE NEXT month and the board members once again trickled into the fellowship hall for a meeting. Both Buford and Maddie looked irate. Dottie glanced secretly at her phone which sat silently on her lap whenever she could. Bob blew his nose, making a surprisingly unusual amount of noise for him.

Sandy seemed to be much more energetic than she had been in a long time. She sat down and swept her blonde bangs out of her face with her hands. Mark and Hubert walked into the meeting wearing big smiles. Mary hurried hastily in, almost banging into another board member's chair, nearly a whole minute late. When she went to sit down she almost missed her chair.

Mark surveyed the board members and then said casually:

"Well, let's get started. We have a lot to go over today."

"Oh, hello Pastor Matthew Love. Can we help you?" asked Sandy.

The rest of the board followed her gaze. Pastor Matthew Love stood in the doorway still dressed in his nice Sunday attire with his baby blue tie hanging over his white shirt almost stiffly straight. He smiled brightly and his eyes were calm and cool as an empty swimming pool.

"I am here for the board meeting."

"Oh, but that isn't necessary, Pastor Matthew Love," said Maddie in a pleasant tone. "You have been doing great work on Sunday mornings and with helping congregants during the week. Why don't you go home and rest."

"Sure," said Mark, cooly. "I've got the meeting under control. Why don't you go watch television."

"Watch television? I can't do that," said Pastor Matthew Love. "I'm the pastor. I must be at all the board meetings. It is my duty to run the church."

"What do you mean you run the church?" asked Buford, incredulously. "You're an android. We, the church board, programmed you to do what we needed you to do. So yes, you can go back into the parsonage and watch television."

The android looked neither agitated nor confused, but continued to speak in its calm manner as if Buford had said nothing that could offend anyone.

"An android? I'm not an android," he said, smiling. "I'm a human, Buford, just like you. I'm Pastor Matthew Love and I'm here to tell people that Jesus loves them."

"Of course, you are," said Mark, bringing over a chair for the android. "We're glad to have you run our church."

"Thank you," answered Pastor Matthew Love as he sat down, not ceasing to smile.

Hubert took a sip of coffee and smiled back at him.

"And don't bother about Buford. He's always making stupid jokes that usually the rest of us don't find funny."

Buford mumbled something nasty under his breath. Maddie cast him a reproachful glance. Mary nervously gulped down what was today her tenth cup of coffee.

"I have been talking to a number of people in the congregation, all of whom have made suggestions for changes they would like to see at our church," said Pastor Matthew Love. "I would like to implement all of them right away."

"Of course," said Hubert, jovially. "Tell us what the congregants want."

"First of all, the congregants want to have mostly fun events at the church, most especially concerts featuring the most popular Christian artists and state of the art light shows. They would also like to remove the first three rows of chairs at the front of the sanctuary to make room for dancing and flash mobs in front of the stage. They would like very short sermons, so that there can be more time for worshipping God in song. The sermons are to all be very happy and to emphasize God's grace. Furthermore, all the congregants I've spoken to agree that the coffee served here every Sunday is disgusting and they would like to have an expensive, imported coffee instead. . ."

The Actually Authentic Android went on like this for over an hour until even Mark and Hubert were annoyed with it.

"Well, if you want to preach short sermons and have more worship in the service, that's fine," said Mark. "But some of those things, like buying that expensive, imported coffee for Sunday mornings, we have to take some time to think over."

"I understand," answered the android. He was no longer smiling, but nevertheless had a genial look upon his face. "Was there any other business to attend to before we bring this board meeting to a close?"

"Yes," replied Maddie without hesitation. "We need to start collecting donations for Thanksgiving. Every Thanksgiving our church gives away twenty-five baskets filled with complete Thanksgiving meals to 25 different needy families in our town. Our church buys the 25 turkeys and the congregants donate the rest of the food and the baskets. Besides the turkey, each basket gets a packet of gravy, a box of stuffing, a can of cranberry jelly, a can of green beans, and a big box of pumpkin pie pudding. A couple of days before Thanksgiving me and a few other volunteers put together the baskets and take them to the families on the list."

"That is a wonderful idea, Maddie," said Pastor Matthew Love, starting to smile again. "We will definitely do that."

"I'll send an email out tonight to the church and post on our social media outlets as well about this," said Sandy.

"Is there any other business to attend to?" asked the android.

Only the android was unannoyed about staying in the meeting so long. Everyone else was fidgety. Mary who was on her fifteenth cup of coffee by now was so jittery that she could not sit still in her seat and even began making her unstable red chair rock back and forth noisily, so that no one except the robot was really able to focus on the meeting. Mark almost grabbed her chair, but thought better of it.

"There is one other piece of business we need to attend to," began Buford.

"What is that?" asked the android, his smile not receding.

"Well, usually about this time we start figuring out a Bible study for Wednesday nights for our home groups to begin a few weeks after the holidays are over. Me, Sandy, and the pastor would always be group home leaders. If we needed another group, we would always have Mary be a group leader too. But we haven't needed a fourth group the last three times. Maddie and whoever is assisting her has a lesson and activities for the children at our church on Wednesday nights while the adults and teens are at the home groups."

"Oh, yes," answered the android. "Members of the congregation have told me about the Wednesday night home groups. Every one of them I've spoken to want it scrapped. They see no point to it. I certainly don't. I'm here to tell people that Jesus loves them. What's a Bible study got to do with that? No, I'm scrapping the Bible study just as the congregation wants."

Buford, Maddie, and even Sandy looked horrified.

But Hubert only chuckled nervously and said:

"Well, whatever you say, pastor."

Mark chimed in his agreement.

"I sure am glad we have you to lead us, Pastor Matthew Love."

Nobody else said anything. Bob put a mint in his mouth. Dottie silently stared down at her phone. Mary was too wired to pay attention.

"Well, if there is nothing else I move to adjourn this meeting," said Pastor Matthew Love. "I understand that there is a possibility of an ice storm tonight. I'm sure none of us want to be out in it."

And without any further discussion, Pastor Matthew Love prayed a brief prayer and everyone got up from the table, Mary being almost as unsteady as some drunk. On her way out, Mary approached the pastor and standing unsteadily she said:

"I just wanted to say pastor that buying that expensive, imported coffee certainly sounds like a wonderful idea. I'm all for it."

And with her wobbling she made her way outside the church.

As soon as Pastor Matthew Love was outside, he wasted no time heading toward the parsonage. It was already raining lightly which was neither normal nor unheard of for October. The weather here always seemed to be unpredictable. One year it had snowed heavily on Halloween, which had led to trick or treating being canceled. This year too on this Halloween night it seemed the children would again miss trick or treating with it already cold and raining and an ice storm threatening to break out upon their town.

Bob, Dottie, and Mary silently headed to their vehicles, Mary nearly slipping as she did so. Mark, making a cowardly dash to his car, came close to slipping himself. But Buford, Maddie, and Sandy circled Hubert before he could hurry off to his expensive, green sports car.

"Hi," said Hubert, smiling nervously. "Shouldn't y'all be getting home? It's already cold and wet out here and remember that ice storm they're all talking about is supposed to come through."

But Sandy stared at him with a hard gaze as did Maddie and Buford.

"We have time, Hubert. None of us live that far away. We need to talk about this."

Hubert did not answer. Suddenly Sandy's face filled with shame. Her frame shook steadily, but not from the cold.

"I was so tired," she said with a sigh. "I was trying to carry out the day-to-day responsibilities of the church and run my business from home. It was getting to be too much. If only my business partner, my husband, was still alive. But that's no excuse. I didn't think this through like I should have. How could I have agreed to make an Actually Authentic Android our pastor and to help program it as Mark, Hubert, and I did? What appalling negligence on our part. And to think that we programmed this thing thinking it would work for us, but now it thinks we work for it. This must not be allowed to continue. We must put a stop to that robot being our pastor."

Hubert chuckled nervously again and stuck his hands inside his coat pockets. He had unfortunately forgotten to wear gloves that day.

"Well, I think it might be premature to retire Matthew Love from being our pastor," said Hubert. "But I suppose we could always make modifications in his programming. I know. Why don't we discuss it at our next board meeting?"

"Are you crazy?" shouted Buford, angrily and incredulously. "Discuss it while that android is there and trying to lead the meeting?"

"How exactly did you, Mark, and Sandy program the Actually Authentic Android, Hubert?" asked Maddie, becoming cross.

Hubert remained silent. He gazed up at the sky and appeared to be studying every aspect and pattern of the clouds. Maddie was not about to be put off and practically shouted at him to answer, but he did not. Then when Maddie had turned her attention back to Sandy, he sneakily slunk off toward his fancy ride.

"Damn fool," barked Buford when he saw him slinking off. "We're never going to get help from him. That's for sure."

"What do we do now?" asked Sandy, looking more fatigued than before they had hired the robot.

"First of all, please tell Buford and I how you programmed the Actually Authentic Android," Maddie said politely.

Sandy seemed to gain a jolt of energy.

"Of course," she answered. "When we programmed the Actually Authentic Android we designed it so that it would react positively to the congregants. If the congregants wanted something, the pastor was to respond in the affirmative. Thus, the congregation in some sense would control the pastor. Also, we programmed the pastor to focus on grace and on Jesus' love. We did not want the pastor to rock the boat in any way."

"So, this pastor is the ultimate people pleaser," observed Buford.

Sandy sighed and shook again, this time from the cold.

"I'm sorry. I've helped to create a real mess here. Look, after the ice storm is over I'll do what I can to reprogram him. Right now, we should all get out of the rain and cold."

Maddie and Buford nodded.

"Agreed. There's no help found in standing out in the rain and cold," said Maddie. "We can fix this situation after the ice storm. I can't imagine even the robot wanting to roam around in such inhospitable weather."

Continuing to shiver, Sandy began the short trek back to her vehicle. Buford began stomping back to his truck. He wore very big boots. Maddie walked a few steps in the direction of her vehicle then suddenly stopped. She turned around and again started walking.

Buford heard a crunching noise behind him and turning around, he was surprised to see Maddie.

"What are you doing?" he asked, flustered. "I thought you were headed home."

He shivered and looked at his truck. Maddie shivered too, but she held her gaze on Buford.

Buford looked back at her with both nervousness and confusion. She did not appear miffed, but she had a serious look upon her face that did not sit well with him. Whatever could she want?

"Buford, I've changed my mind. I think we should shut the robot down today."

His nervousness and confusion left him and instead his whole manner suggested determination. Even the cold rain seemed not to faze him.

"I agree, Maddie. You know I never liked the idea of that thing running loose. Let's meet back here in an hour. I need to go home and get a few things."

Maddie smiled.

"Alright. I'll see then."

Both of them were mulling over what they must do as they took off in their separate vehicles. They had to drive slower than usual, but neither Buford nor Maddie was going to let rain or even ice keep them from their goal.

Chapter 5

The Rebellion

THE RAIN, THE FREEZING rain had been falling on and off for a couple of hours. The sound of cars was seldom heard outside. Thunder rumbled louder than a bowling ball felling the pins in a strike. Lightning flashed like ghosts in the blackened stormy sky. No animal could be heard stirring outside. No person wanted to be, but two were out there whether they ought to have been or not.

Buford was bundled up in so many clothes that barely more than his eyes were visible. Maddie maintained a similar attire, albeit flashier, including very high hot pink snow boots.

"Well, I'll be glad when we're done here," he said. "I don't want to be out when the ice gets bad."

"I know," agreed Maddie. "Hey how come you got a gun?"

Buford was holding a revolver in one hand and a couple of bullets in another. He loaded it, aimed it at a tree, but did not fire.

"Well, I figured that I could hold the gun on him while you turn him off."

"I doubt that gun will damage him," answered Maddie, a bit incredulously. "Remember the ad said he was virtually indestructible."

"Yes. But he doesn't know that," Buford said, grinning. "Remember. He thinks he's human."

"That's right," exclaimed Maddie. "So, we can use that to our advantage."

"Exactly," said Buford. "Now let's get into the pastor's house. We just need to figure out how to get in. Unfortunately, Hubert has the only extra key to the place."

"Well, why not just knock on the front door," suggested Maddie. "Maybe the robot will let us in."

"Good thinking," said Buford, baffled as to why he hadn't thought of that.

Buford put the gun and the other bullet into one of his coat pockets. Then he and Maddie began heading toward the parsonage. As they walked, rain continued to pelt everything as if launching an assault on earth. A light was on in the living room, and after they had stepped onto the unelaborate covered porch, Maddie reached out one of her hands gloved in pink and knocked hard and loud upon the door to ensure that the Actually Authentic Android would hear it.

No answer immediately happened. The cold rain suddenly grew harder and noisier. A wind blew beneath the porch like a cunning thief, trying to steal Maddie's hat off her head, but she grabbed it just in time. Then she turned again to the dark brown mundane door and it opened.

There was no surprise in the expression of the Actually Authentic Android. He smiled as pleasantly as ever, his eyes seemingly locked onto some serene portrait quite a contrast from the wild raging tempest outside.

"Well, Buford, Maddie, what are you doing outside on a night like this? Is something wrong?" While he asked these things his expression did not change a bit. Neither Buford nor Maddie knew how to answer the robot. They hadn't really planned to talk to it. Momentarily, Buford forgot the loaded gun in his pocket.

"Please, come in friends," said Pastor Matthew Love, smiling even more, if such a thing were possible.

Maddie gazed at the pastor with apprehension. Bright and pleasant as his smile was, she had begun to find it creepy. Was there anything behind this smile? Surely, it was no more than a programed response. Surely, no android, even a so-called Actually Authentic Android, could really feel glad to see them or genuinely care about their well-being. And what of him or rather it? Did it have any right to object if she and Buford were to put it out of commission?

The Actually Authentic Android led them into his living room where they sat down on his sofa.

"Please, make yourselves at home, friends," he said. "I have a pot of coffee on. I'll bring you each a cup. And cookies."

"Thank you," said Buford and Maddie together.

When Pastor Matthew Love was gone from sight Maddie cast a confused look over at Buford.

"The Actually Authentic Android just said he made coffee. Can an android drink coffee? And can it eat cookies?"

Baffled, Buford said: "I don't know."

"He really does think he's human," said Maddie, perplexed. "When he comes back we really must find a way to shut him down."

"We will," answered Buford, resolutely. "But first we should try to loll the android into a false sense of security. It's a computer. It expects us to do what's logical and predictable."

"So, we start by being totally predictable and then we surprise it," finished Maddie with a triumphant smile.

"Exactly," said Buford. "Listen. Here comes Pastor Matthew Love. Remember. Let's be intentional."

"Right," asserted Maddie.

Pastor Matthew Love came into the living room carrying a tray with three cups of coffee, three spoons, a pile of napkins, a container of sugar, a container of cream, and three little plates bearing two oatmeal raisin cookies apiece. He set the tray upon the coffee table. He pulled the rocking chair closer to the table, and sitting down in it, he began to rock steadily.

Maddie picked up a cookie and bit into it.

"Mmm. This is delicious," she said, pleasantly. "Thank you."

"Yeah. Thanks," blurted Buford, and then took a sip of coffee. Buford liked his coffee black.

"You're welcome," said the Actually Authentic Android, gazing at them with his typical smile, although he seemed to be concentrating more on his rocking than on them. It was so methodical and Maddie was sure that she could count 4-beat measures as the robot rocked away.

"Now why did you both come here tonight, especially in such terrible weather?" asked Pastor Matthew Love, not ceasing his rhythmic rocking as he spoke.

Maddie gazed a moment at Buford, hoping he would answer first and just in case he hesitated she took a scene out of Bob's playbook, taking a big bite of cookie. Buford thought it best not to copy her. He took a sip of coffee and looking the Actually Authentic Android in the eye he said very causally:

"Well, we were just passing through and we thought we'd just stop by and see how you were doing, this being your first time in a bad storm like this and all."

"That's right," chimed in Maddie. "You know sometimes when we get a freezing rain like this a lot of ice forms on the ground and on the trees. Tree branches break and cause a lot of damage, and even sometimes death. Sometimes the power goes out too, for hours or even days, and it can get scary sitting in the dark all alone. Especially so with how the parsonage sits on such a lonely road that gets little traffic."

"Oh, how very kind of you," answered Pastor Matthew Love, continuing to rock. "I assure you though that I am just fine. I have just been enjoying some coffee and cookies."

"Glad to hear that," said Buford, wryly. "Though we do have one question."

"What's that?" asked the android, neither ceasing his smiling nor his rocking.

"How can a robot enjoy coffee and cookies?" asked Buford, sounding baffled.

"Yeah. How can a robot even drink coffee and eat cookies?" asked Maddie, giving the robot a hard, suspicious look.

The robot's rocking immediately stopped, but his smile did not lessen.

"Why do you two think I'm a robot?" asked the robot. "You know that I'm your pastor, Pastor Matthew Love and I'm here to tell you that Jesus loves you."

"Of course, you are," answered Maddie with a hint of sarcasm. "That's just what Hubert, Mark, and Sandy programmed you for."

Pastor Matthew Love showed no sign that this statement affected him in the slightest. Nothing changed in his functional features.

"But I'm not a robot, friends. I'm human."

"Well, let's test that, shall we?" answered Buford, bluntly, pulling out his gun and pointing it at Pastor Matthew Love.

Finally, faded the smile upon Pastor Matthew Love's face. But when he spoke there was neither a hint of confusion nor of fear. His voice remained steadily monotone.

"Now what's this? Do you mean to shoot me? I have done nothing to either of you."

Neither board member answered the android, but both Buford and Maddie laughed heartily for half a minute.

"What is it you want?," continued the robot. "Have you come to rob me?"

"No. We've come to assassinate you," shouted Maddie, menacingly. "You've been preaching about how Jesus Christ gives us eternal life. You want to experience it? You want to go meet him?"

"But for what reason!" shouted the robot. "What could you possibly gain by it?"

"Shut up!" shouted Buford, aiming the gun at Pastor Matthew Love's head. "Although I suppose it is a shame to kill him before picking his pockets. Go ahead, Maddie."

"Yes. Please pick my pockets, but don't kill me," shouted the robot all the more, although somehow he could not manage to sound fearful. "Or why don't I just give you what's in them and then you can leave."

Pastor Matthew Love had raised his arms over his head. Now he began to lower them. But Buford cocked his gun.

"Hey! Don't move," blared Buford. "Maddie will pick your pockets and then we'll decide whether to leave you alive or not. We're in charge here. Got it, pastor!"

Pastor Matthew Love quickly put his arms back over his head and stood as still as he could.

"I can tell you already," he explained in a matter-of-fact manner, "that you will not find much to steal in my pockets. In the right front pocket of my pants are my keys. In the left front pocket of my pants is a pack of gum. It has five sticks, never been opened. I've already taken everything out of my back pockets. My cellphone was in my back pocket on my right side this morning. It's in good condition. My wallet was in my back pocket on my left side this morning. It contains my state I.D., my social security card, three credit cards, and five dollars and forty-five cents. Pastors don't make that much."

"Shut up, pastor!" shouted Maddie.

"Yes. Shut him up, Maddie, so we can get out of here," said Buford. "I'm sure it's getting colder out there"

"What do you mean 'shut me up'?" asked the android.

"You'll see soon enough," Maddie chimed cryptically.

Maddie began to walk over to Pastor Matthew Love. The pastor did not so much as turn around. He did not speak for a bit and he actually frowned. Maddie came up to his back side. First she put a hand into the right pocket of his pants and grasping his keys, she pulled them out.

"I'll take those," she said, stuffing them into her own pants pocket. "You can keep your gum."

"But I want the gum," blurted Buford

Maddie grabbed it roughly out of the pastor's pants' pocket.

"Here you go, Buford," she said, tossing it to him.

Buford caught it in his free hand.

"Thanks."

Maddie made a wry smile.

"Well, now I guess all there is left to do is silence you."

"You mean. . .?" began the robot.

"Yes. That's right. Say good-bye to your life," said Buford, laughing in a cruel manner.

But as Buford laughed he absentmindedly shot off the gun. The bullet hit the robot right in the chest and then went flying right back at Buford. The android put his arms down, stared at the bullet hole in his Sunday shirt, and then at Buford lying down on the floor. He was bleeding from his chest and not moving.

"I really am a robot, aren't I?" Pastor Matthew Love said slowly. "How else could a bullet hit me in the chest and I not be dead?"

Then he became aware that a hand was moving his hair behind his head. He quickly turned around and gazed straight at Maddie.

"And just what were you trying to do, Maddie?" inquired the robot. Then he felt around in the hair on the back of his head. "Ah. Yes. I see now what you were up to."

Maddie made to run off, but Pastor Matthew Love grabbed her by the throat.

"You really did mean to kill me, didn't you?" he said. "So, tell me, does the whole church know I'm a robot."

"No," squeaked Maddie. "Only the board."

She tried in desperation to escape his grip, but there was no overpowering the Actually Authentic Android. It stared at her, smiling as widely as ever.

"Hello. I'm Pastor Matthew Love and I'm here to tell you that Jesus loves you. Wouldn't you like to meet Jesus, Maddie?"

"Wait. Stop," said Maddie weakly as the android slowly began to apply pressure on her neck. Another minute and her arms hung limp in the air. Pastor Matthew Love let her drop to the floor and then stared down at both bodies.

"I must act quickly," droned the android. "These two came for me. The rest of the church board is sure to come after me. But first I must take care of these bodies. I know. There is a cemetery behind the church. I will bury them there."

Pastor Matthew Love studied the carpet closely.

"I hope I can get the blood out."

Chapter 6

Dottie Dies

Pastor Matthew Love stood in the cemetery shoveling mud over a new unmarked grave. He was still dressed in his Sunday best, but even with the cold rain pelting him he did not shiver. Neither did his body show any signs of rusting. Surprisingly, a crow sat perched up in a tree near him. It cawed loudly, but he did not pay the creature any mind. Nothing, not even the harsh elements had any bearing on his ability to complete his task. For a human it would have amounted to a strenuous and repetitive task, but for a robot it was neither. When he had finished covering over the grave he surveyed it silently and then walked to the parsonage. He put the shovel back in the closet and then sat at his desk.

"And now I must find the rest of the church board before they come find me."

His clothes were still wet and even dirty. But he had at least managed not to get any blood on them. The bloodstains which had been on the carpet were no longer there or at least their traces were dreadfully difficult to notice. The robot had used the best means to clean possible which were to be procured by the small array of items to be found in the small parsonage closet. The smile on his face did not fade. No fear was found in his features. His programming did not allow for it.

"Yes. I know where all the board members are," droned the android. "I have all their addresses. I have a GPS to find them. I will go to Dottie's house first. Yes. Dottie's house is nearest. It's only 3 blocks away."

Rising the robot went to the closet. He grabbed some rope which he slung over his shoulder. Then he reached into his pocket. His fingers found Buford's revolver inside his pocket. He had already loaded it with the extra bullet.

Time to go," he said in a deadpan way.

◆ ◆ ◆

It was below freezing outside and already ice was forming on the trees and powerlines as Dottie sat on her sofa wrapped up in her favorite blanket which was covered with pictures of poltergeists, holding a hot cup of tea in her left hand, both sides of her cup bearing a picture of a vampire with a caption underneath him reading: "Can I please borrow a cup of blood?" She was watching her new favorite show on her favorite streaming site, a paranormal romance called *The Naked and the Bloodthirsty*. This was the fifth episode in a row she had watched tonight and she showed no signs of becoming bored with the show. In fact, her interest could not be more pronounced. Her eyes stood still, staring at the screen, and she was leaning forward. It seemed nothing could peel her eyes from the screen. . .except for Patience.

Patience was eight years old and the only child of Dottie and her ex husband, Charles. Charles lived on the other side of town and had ceased coming to their church after the divorce. Dottie and Charles took turns taking Patience in monthly installments, barely saying a word to one another when one of them would pick her up or drop her off. In fact, both would hardly talk to Patience when she was in their care. She had taken to keeping her cat with her when she was at either of her parents' homes. She would speak to her cat, Mr. Swabs, as if he were her best friend. Indeed, she really didn't have any friends. But on this stormy night, he had wandered from her sight, and she was distressfully looking for him. Thus, it was for this reason that she came into the living room still being dressed in her witch costume.

"Mommy," she said as entered the room.

But Dottie did not move or show any sign that she had heard her daughter.

"Mommy. Mommy," repeated Patience, somewhat louder than before.

But still Dottie only stared at the television, seemingly unaware that anyone was in the room with her.

"Mommy! Mommy!" shouted Patience, distressed.

"What?!" shouted Dottie, angrily, pausing her program. Then she said in a growling voice: "Don't shout Patience. I've told you so many times. I can hear you fine without you shouting. Now why are you troubling me? Can't you see that I'm in the middle of something? Now what is it you want?"

"I can't find Mr. Swabs," said Patience, beginning to cry.

Her mother sighed with fiery irritation.

"Patience. Stop crying. You're much too old for that. Think. Mr. Swabs is in the house somewhere. You just haven't looked hard enough. Now you go look for him and leave me alone. Got it?"

"Yes, mommy," replied Patience, miserably, tears streaming from her eyes.

She knew it was pointless to say more so she left the living room in silence more quickly than she had entered it. Dottie let out another sigh of annoyance, but just as she was about to turn on her show again, there came a knock on the front door.

"Yes! Who is it?!" shouted Dottie, not bothering to hide her irritation. Dottie quickly got up, opened the door, and suddenly she smiled, embarrassed.

"Oh sorry, Pastor Matthew Love. How can I help you? Please come in."

The robot, smiling back, stepped into her home.

◆ ◆ ◆

Patience had walked back to her room, crestfallen. She had never had trouble finding Mr. Swabs before and she had already looked all over the house for him. She wondered if perhaps he had found his way out into the icy storm outside. She knew if she bundled up and went outside, her mother would never be the wiser. She had just grasped her overcoat from out of her walk-in closet and was about to put it on when suddenly she heard a gentle sound behind her and felt something soft rub against her leg.

"Oh, Mr. Swabs!" she exclaimed when she had turned around.

Mr. Swabs looked up at her and meowed. Patience peered under her bed where she kept numerous board games that nobody played in dusty little stacks and the dust on Mr. Swabs' pretty coat, and she immediately realized where he had been.

"Were you taking a nap, Mr. Swabs?" Patience asked when she had picked him up. The soft cat meowed at her and did not struggle. She began making her way back to the living room, carrying the cat.

"Now I can show mommy that I found you," she said eagerly.

◆ ◆ ◆

When Patience came close to the living room, but it was still blocked from her view, noise from her mother's television show came upon her ears. Her mother had been angry with her last time she had interrupted her show, perhaps she had best not bother to show her the cat. She stopped for a moment, considering turning back. But then she went on.

"I won't interrupt her show. I'll just hold up Mr. Swabs and show her that I found him."

She went on confidently, but when the living room came into view she stopped. Clutching her cat close to her she screamed and her tears fell again fiercely. Her mother's body dangled in the air and did not move. Outside the ice storm grew more tempestuous. Suddenly, the television went blank, while at the same time the house became completely dark. The wrath of the ice storm had begun and the wrath of the robot went on.

Chapter 7

Mary's Mania

MARY WAS SHAKING CRAZILY all over as she carried her coffee into the kitchen, coming close to spilling it several times. She had wanted to go to bed early because it was piercingly cold in her house without the heater on, but she knew she would never be able to sleep. The power was still off, but thanks to her stove being gas, and her windup lanterns she was still able to make instant coffee. This one was French vanilla flavored and super strong, almost twice as strong as what she was accustomed to drinking at church on Sunday mornings and at board mornings. Mary was most certainly wired much more that the powerlines outside when they worked.

Mary had already piled eight blankets onto her ragged, red couch. She had thermals under her coffee themed pajamas. She was just about to set her coffee down on the table in front of her couch and to settle down in her warm cocoon when suddenly there came a knock at the door. Mary was so startled that she sent drops of coffee from her coffee themed cup onto her coffee themed floor. Putting on her light brown robe she bouncily crept toward the door and put an eye up to the peep hole. Then she hastily opened the door so that it slammed against the wall dangerously and with high volume.

Pastor Matthew Love stood on Mary's porch smiling at her. Mary felt like a motor that wouldn't turn off even as she only stood, staring at the robot. She tried to focus her attention upon him, but her mind seemed to race in two different directions.

"Hello, Mary. May I please come in?" intoned the Actually Authentic Android.

"Why of course, pastor," anxiously answered Mary. "Can I get you some coffee?"

"Yes. Thank you," answered the Actually Authentic Android insipidly, and then entered Mary's house.

"Please sit and have a seat on a chair in the living room," Mary said shakily.

Mary went over to a cupboard in her kitchen and took out a coffee cup. This cup featured a man looking at a dog suspiciously and there was a thought cloud coming from the dog which read: "How would I know what's become of the cat?" Then she scooped instant coffee into the cup and poured hot water over it.

"Would you like sugar and creamer in your coffee, pastor?"

"Yes, please," Pastor Matthew Love answered automatically.

Mary then poured non-dairy creamer and sugar into the coffee cup, stirred up the coffee, and brought the cup over to the pastor. He took it from her hand.

"Thank you, Mary."

"You're welcome."

Mary set to winding the lantern on the coffee table so that it wouldn't go out. Then she grabbed her own coffee cup and sat down on the sofa. She proceeded to gulp down her coffee quickly, while the robot sipped his own in a seemingly methodical manner.

"So now how can I help you, pastor?" inquired Mary when she had finished her coffee.

The pastor was still sipping his coffee in some kind of intentional manner. He did not respond right away, but after a minute he finally said:

"Mary, where is Mike this evening?"

"Oh, were you wanting to talk to him about something important? I'm afraid that he left this afternoon for a business trip. He won't be back until late Saturday night."

"You mean he left you all alone here and in this terrible weather. I can't believe he would drive when the roads are all slippery with ice."

"Of course, my husband wouldn't drive in these conditions. He took a taxi. And anyway, I am perfectly able to take care of myself even in an ice storm with the power out. This is really nothing compared to the ice storm we had twelve years ago. We had to cancel trick or treating on Halloween that year too. My husband will be just fine. I am glad he will have a chance to check on our son, Benny, before he gets home. Benny just started college this Fall."

"I am glad to hear that," replied the robot.

Although Mary had trouble focusing on the robot's face, she could still sense sterileness in the robot's features: its' smile that seemed painted on his face, its' blank eyes. Despite its' encouraging words, their monotone delivery prevented them from sounding empathetic.

"But please tell me, Pastor Matthew Love, why did you come here tonight and in this terrible weather?"

Then perplexment showed clearly upon her face. Momentarily, she found herself able to focus, although her heart rate ran like a runner at a track meet.

"How did you get here anyway? I didn't hear you drive up."

"That's because I didn't drive, Mary," answered the android. "I walked here."

Mary stared at him, becoming more perplexed.

"But that's a mile away. And you're not even wearing a coat. And you didn't seem cold at all standing out there."

"Ah. But androids don't get cold, Mary."

Mary gasped. Her surprise and shock were evident in her face.

"I am an android, aren't I, Mary?"

His smile held, but somehow Mary continued to feel that his eyes seemed blank as they gazed back at her.

"That's why you wanted to talk, isn't it? How did you find out that you're an android?"

There was no change in the robot's countenance.

"Buford and Maddie told me," replied Pastor Matthew Love. "They came to the parsonage this afternoon to turn me off. That is what the board plans to do, isn't Mary? To shut me off for good?"

"What?! No!" answered Mary. "Look. I don't know what Buford and Maddie thought they were doing, but none of the other board members, including me, want to shut you down. We hired you to be our pastor. You're. . ."

"Pastor Matthew Love," interrupted the robot. "And I'm here to tell you that Jesus loves you. You do want to see Jesus, don't you Mary? Like Buford and Maddie and Dottie are seeing Jesus?"

Mary looked horrified and recoiled in her seat as her heart raced more now from fear than from coffee.

"You killed them. You're a murderer. You've come here to murder me."

The robot continued to smile at her as if they were having a pleasant conversation.

"I'm not a murderer," replied the robot. "I'm only killing those who would murder me. And I only killed two of them. One of them killed themselves."

Mary made to stand up.

"Don't move, Mary," said Pastor Matthew Love, cocking Buford's gun, which he was now holding.

Mary hurled her coffee cup at the robot and ran, but he was too quick. There was a bang and Mary dropped to the floor, bleeding from her head. Pastor Matthew Love grabbed his coffee cup and sipped the rest of his coffee. Then he gazed down at Mary's body.

"Four down. Four to go."

Chapter 8

Hubert's High

HUBERT YAWNED AND ONCE again dipped his hand into his bag of pork rinds. He sat all alone in the dark on his maroon couch, which was so old and worn that it was flat more than cushy. As it thundered outside and ice fell from the trees Hubert looked as though he couldn't care less. He looked like he was in a trance as he mechanically ate his pork rinds as if he also were a robot, one programed to eat pork rinds.

When he had completed his task he tossed away the bag into the darkness, marveling to himself what a nice sound it made as it crumpled away. Then he moved his hands around the table clumsily. For a few minutes his hands would keep finding what they were looking for, but then drop them. Each time Hubert would act nonchalant and try again even more clumsily. Finally, Hubert held his lighter in one hand and another joint in the other. For another minute he fiddled with both of them, coming close a couple of times to lighting his hand on fire, all the while never seeming to realize this danger.

When he had lit his joint Hubert nearly set his couch on fire with his lit lighter, but turned it off at the last second. Hubert took a puff of his joint and a wave of euphoria washed over his face despite the redness of his usually auburn eyes.

At that moment, there came a couple of knocks at the door, but Hubert showed no sign that he had heard them. He stared blankly across the room and continued to puff his joint. Twice again came the knock upon the door.

"Ha. Ha. Knock. Knock," Hubert squeaked stupidly, knocking on the table twice.

This time there came three knocks upon the door.

"Knock. Knock. Knock," Hubert again squeaked stupidly, knocking three times upon the table.

The knocking upon the door again came in a pattern of three.

"Huh.? What's that?" asked Hubert in the same stupid squeak.

This time he did not answer back by knocking on the table. He listened, continuing quietly to puff his joint. The three knocks came again upon the door.

"Ha. Ha. Ah. Yes. There's someone at the door," squeaked Hubert. "I will go to the door and see who it is."

Putting the joint into his mouth he stood, and slowly walked over to the door. Two more choruses of three knocks on the door came before he reached his destination. Hubert opened the door and a euphoric smile spread across his face. He took his joint out of his mouth.

"Oh. Hi pastor. How are you doing?"

He took a few puffs from his joint, which floated right into Pastor Matthew Love's face. The pastor did not cough or complain, but he only smiled and remained silent. It took Hubert a whole minute to realize what he had done.

"Oh, sorry, pastor," he said, in a mildly embarrassed tone of voice. "I'll just get rid of this."

Hubert made to toss his joint, but carelessly dropped it instead. Hubert laughed this off. Pastor Matthew Love made note of where the joint fell. Then he turned his attention again to Hubert.

"Well, I don't ordinarily smoke," explained Hubert, heartily. "But I thought it was fitting on such a cold night as this."

"Oh, I quite understand," answered Pastor Matthew Love.

"Well, anyway, how can I help you?" asked Hubert, his embarrassment having disappeared and his smile widely spreading.

"Oh, it wasn't much," answered Pastor Matthew Love, smiling back. "I just wondered if I could borrow a lighter from you. I think I would like a smoke too."

"Of course, pastor," answered Hubert, happily. Then chuckling, he added to himself: "A robot wants a smoke. Well, who would have thought."

He wandered nonchalantly further into his house and a few minutes later came back with a purple lighter. Hubert handed it to the robot.

"Here ya go, pastor. And don't worry about bringing it back. I've got six more."

"Oh, thank you," answered Pastor Matthew Love. "Hopefully, this weather improves soon. See you at church next Sunday?"

Hubert continued to smile.

"Sure thing, pastor. Well, nighty night now."

"Yes. Nighty night now," responded the robot.

Then Hubert closed the door, leaving Pastor Matthew Love on his covered wooden porch. There was light on the porch because Pastor Matthew Love had brought one of Mary's lanterns with him. The pastor stood silently gazing at the purple lighter in his hand. Then he quietly clicked it on and kneeling down, he lit the dry wood of the porch, and then dropped the open lighter on it. Near the door, Hubert's discarded lit joint smoked. The robot stepped off the porch.

"This goal of mine is becoming too easy," said Pastor Matthew Love. "Humans truly are irrational creatures."

And having said this, he wandered off into the cold darkness.

Chapter 9

Mark's Misstep

As the storm continued to rage outside, Amber had just put on her blue, warm fleece robe as she stood by the bed. Her husband, Mitch, had gone to visit her parents. Mark's wife, Elaine, had gone to Chicago for work. Amber smiled to herself while she found her blue, warm fleece slippers and put them on over her smooth feet with toenails painted to match her robe perfectly, as were her painted fingernails. To top it all off, Amber pulled on her blue scrunchy, arranging her beautiful brown hair into the perfect ponytail. Even her lively, happy eyes were painted around with blue eyeshadow and her perfume's scent sailed through the air, making the room smell of blueberries.

Mark meanwhile had already pulled on his underwear, his blue jeans, his bright orange shirt, and a sweater with a busy design. He had also put on a thick coat because it was cold inside the house. On his feet he wore thin white socks, but over these he wore fleece black and white slippers, which were ugly and bland.

He was now in the kitchen trying to figure out how he could put together a meal with the power being out. Mark unlike Mary did not have a gas stove. Fortunately, Mark found that the pipes had not frozen and there was running water. Mark filled two mugs with hot water and then put a tea bag of Earl Grey in each. Then he found a can of smoked meat and opening it, took out the meat, sliced it into slabs and put two each of the rectangular slabs between two slices of bread, making four sandwiches. Mark had just set the two mugs of hot tea and two plates with two sandwiches each on the table when there came a knocking on the front door.

"Hmm. I wonder who that could be," Mark muttered to himself. "Who'd be crazy enough to be out in this weather?"

The knocking came again and approaching the door, Mark opened it.

"Pastor Matthew Love? Is something wrong? What are you doing here?"

Pastor Matthew Love was standing on the red brick covered porch, smiling, holding one of Mary's lanterns in his hand with the cold rain pouring down in the background.

Mark, still puzzled, motioned for the pastor to come inside.

"Please. Have a seat in the kitchen. I'll be back in a moment."

Mark picked up one of the teas and one of the plates of sandwiches and wandered back into the bedroom where Amber was now standing, wearing another one of Mark's heavy coats over her robe, looking as lovely as ever.

"What is it? Who was at the door?" she asked in a sultry voice.

"It's only Pastor Matthew Love," answered Mark, trying to hide how anxious he was at that moment. "I'm not sure why he is here. But I wanted to warn you to stay out of sight. I'll get him out of here as soon as I can. Here's your dinner."

"Thank you," Amber said sweetly.

Mark set the tea and the plate of sandwiches on the table by his wife's side of the bed. Then he left to return to the kitchen.

Pastor Matthew Love was sitting on a stool in the kitchen staring at Elaine's expensive knife set. He didn't immediately look up at Mark when he entered the room. Mark still pondered what the robot wanted and why he had come to his house in such terrible weather. Surely a robot would exhibit more logic than to go out into an ice storm! But then again, perhaps not. Mark only knew that he had to get the pastor to leave. Mark strode up to him, trying to be as casual as possible.

"So, pastor what can I help you with?" he asked, forcing a good-natured looking smile.

Pastor Matthew Love immediately stood up and walked over to Elaine's expensive knife set.

"What a lovely knife set," exclaimed the pastor.

"Why, thank you, pastor," answered Mark, majestically. "I bought it for my wife last Christmas. She's been very pleased with it."

"Wonderful to hear," said Pastor Matthew Love in monotone. Then he pulled one of the knives out of its slot and looked at it. "Hmm. Do you have any idea what this knife is used for, Mark?"

Mark stared at the knife and shook his head.

"I have no idea, pastor."

"It's a paring knife," answered the android, glancing only momentarily at Mark. Then the robot replaced the paring knife into its slot and pulled out another knife.

"What about this knife?" he asked. "What do you do with it?"

"Uh," began Mark, becoming more confused every moment.

"It's a bread knife. She's a beauty, isn't she?" said Pastor Matthew Love, looking admiringly at it before putting it back in its slot. Then he pulled out still another knife. "And what do you suppose this one is used for?"

Mark was no longer only confused. He was irritated and he did not even try to hide it.

"I have no idea, pastor. These are Elaine's knives, not mine. But I can assure you. . ." and opening a drawer he pulled out a utensil, "that I know this is a butter knife."

"Ah. Yes, indeed," answered the android. "Well, this is a steak knife. But I imagine that it is good for more than just slicing steak. Wouldn't you say so, Mark?"

"Well, I have no reason to think otherwise."

"Perhaps helpful to cut a squirrel into pieces?" asked the pastor.

Mark wasn't sure what to say. He still could not understand what the robot wanted, but he wished for the first time that the contraption would get lost. But before he had long to contemplate this, he fell over onto the floor with a pained cry, blood streaming on his shirt.

"And a very good choice for killing you just as I predicted," said the robot without a hint of emotion. Then he stared at the knife and next down at Mark. Then equally emotionlessly he said:

"You human beings are so unintelligent. You don't even know what all your own knives are for."

Then he replaced the knife and walked out of the kitchen.

◆ ◆ ◆

Amber sat in her sedan, praying that it would start. It was still icy and cold outside, although the rain had quit falling for the moment. She hadn't bothered to eat the food or drink the tea, which Mark had brought to her. Instead, she had quickly changed into her clothes. She was bundled up in thermals, a sweatsuit with her head covered by the sweatshirt hood, and thick wool gloves. She had also donned thick wool socks and heavy black snow boots. Over her thermals and sweat outfit she wore two coats: one of her own and one of Mark's. As soon as she'd dressed, she stealthily sneaked out of the sliding door which led out of the master bedroom where she was. Then she had gone out the backyard gate quietly, trying as she might to stay out of sight of the front of the house.

She knew that once she started the car and got the heat going that she would be sweating, but she did not dare remove either of the coats. She wanted to get away as quickly as she could manage.

She put her key into the ignition and turned it. The car started. She was beyond relieved and immediately she began to back out into the street. She didn't bother to turn her camera on or look behind her. She thought it absurd that anything or anyone would be behind her in the street.

But as the sedan rolled back it suddenly slammed into something, stopping, and sending Amber almost into her windshield. She hadn't bothered to put on her seatbelt. She didn't bother to try to figure out what she'd hit, but she turned off her car and grabbed her purse. Before she could get out of the vehicle, a familiar face appeared at her window. Amber rolled it down.

"Pastor Matthew Love. Hi," she said, nervously.

The pastor gazed at Amber and smiled.

"Ah. Amber. You're one of the nursery workers at our church, aren't you?"

Amber nodded, trying not to show the extent of her nervousness. She tried to smile back at the pastor, unsure if it would come across naturally enough.

"Now what might you be doing visiting Mark Stamos this evening and in such dreadful weather?" asked the android.

Amber blurted out the first thing that came to her mind.

"Oh. I just thought I'd drop by and check on Elaine. She and I are great friends and I don't live far from her."

"Oh really? Because I thought you came here to see Mark."

Amber's smile disappeared and she looked crestfallen.

"Now Amber you do want to tell your pastor all about it, don't you?"

◆ ◆ ◆

Mark lay bleeding on the floor fighting to keep conscious, fumbling for his phone in his coat pocket. Finally getting his phone onto the kitchen floor, he unlocked it with the code, and hitting the contact he wanted, he listened as the other person's phone rang, hoping he would survive long enough to speak to them. It had not even been a minute when the contact picked up and a familiar voice said:

"Hello."

Mark did not dare switch the phone to speaker, but instead slithered as close as he could to the phone and shouted:

"Sandy!"

"Hi Mark. What is it you want?" she asked, sounding slightly annoyed. "Look. My phone is about to die and I can't charge it. I really can't talk now."

"Sandy! Listen!" Mark shouted, frantically. "The robot stabbed me! I'm dying! He's sure to come for you! You need to go! Flee!"

"What?! Pastor Matthew Love?!" shouted Sandy in disbelief.

"Go Sandy! Go now!" Mark shouted in a voice of utter desperation.

Then Mark heard footsteps on the kitchen floor. He could not see who made them, but nevertheless he knew who did.

"What's this, Mark? Still alive?" said Pastor Matthew Love in monotone. "Well, I will have to use a different knife now, won't I?

Without another word the robot grasped another knife out of Elaine's fancy set.

"Mark! Mark!" shouted Sandy.

Then suddenly she heard a loud pained scream in her ear through her phone.

"Mark! Mark!" she shouted.

But there was silence on the other end. Then Sandy's phone went dead.

"Crap. This is what I get for forgetting to charge my phone overnight and spending most of the day on social media," she said angrily to herself.

She took a long, anxious breath.

"I've got to hurry. That robot isn't far away."

Meanwhile Pastor Matthew Love had picked up Mark's phone.

"Ah. Yes. You called Sandy," he said to himself, emotionlessly. "Now what will you do? Try to escape? Amber couldn't escape from me. Or will you come after me? The board is out to put me out of commission after all. But no matter. I'll get you, Sandy, and mute Bob too."

Then violently he stuck Elaine's knife back into its slot.

Chapter 10

Sandy's Sanity is Questioned

SANDY FELT AWFUL. WHY had she ever voted to make a robot their pastor? How many board members had this contraption already killed? She did not waste time getting a lot of things together. She immediately piled clothes upon her body and stormed out into the cold, not caring how ridiculously her clothing choices clashed or that she had accidently put on her late husband's old snow boots instead of her own. She didn't even bother to lock her door, but stepped into her silver pickup.

There was only a light drizzle of rain, but everywhere ice caked the tree branches. She was afraid some of the branches might break off and fall onto her. She quickly turned the key in the ignition, backed out of the driveway, and sped down the street.

As she expected, the street was totally dark, and everyone was inside. Neither the moon nor stars could be seen. Only the bright beams of her eyelike headlights could be seen.

Sandy wanted to speed up and get out of the city limits as soon as possible, but she did not dare. Even though she was an experienced driver and had a good vehicle with new tires and with chains on them she did not want to risk skidding off the road or crashing into something. She hoped that by not taking the most logical route out of town, the robot would not find her.

Sandy's plan was to drive to the next town over, which was a considerable distance away, and hide out in a hotel there. Then after a couple of days she would drive to the next state and stay with her sister. She wished she could warn the other board members, if any were still alive, but she could think of no way to warn them without putting her own life in danger. Once she was safely across state lines with her sister, she would inform the congregation that their pastor was a robot.

"I'll have to buy a new cell phone," she thought. "Otherwise, I am sure that thing can track me. Perhaps it's a good thing my phone died."

After about twenty minutes, Sandy passed a small shopping center to her left. All the lights of the businesses were out, and to her surprise one car sat in the parking lot of a restaurant.

"I guess I shouldn't be too surprised that the police are out," said Sandy to herself. "I wonder if perhaps I ought to talk to them."

But she decided against this and drove on. Afterall, how would the police stop Pastor Matthew Love. Usually, the street Sandy was driving down was busy, but at this time of night and in this weather it was completely empty.

After another couple of minutes, Sandy turned to the left, and went down a slender side street. This road was every bit as empty as the other, but it was darker and lined with disheveled houses. Sandy was sure that either no one lived on this street or they must be very poor or very shady.

She was getting much closer to the edge of town. She thought it best not to take one of the main roads to leave town. The quieter her departure the better. Sandy sighed. Only ten miles or so and she would be out of town and on her way to one about ten times the size. As she continued she wondered why she had stayed in this town for so long. Sure it had a few people who were her friends, but her best and most beloved friend was gone. Her husband, William, had died of cancer five years ago. Since then, Sandy had engrossed herself in running their business and running the church in an unacknowledged attempt to keep her mind off her own loneliness. But in the end this only made her tired. Now tearing herself from both business and church, she drove upon a lonely, thin road, reminded of her own inner loneliness that she had tried hard to hide, to deny, but the dread that she had anticipated at finally acknowledging it did not come. Instead, with the revelation of the truth of her own emotion, she felt at peace.

Again, Sandy sighed. The rain picked up. It pelted hard against her strong vehicle. Sandy was grateful she was out of the rain, grateful for the warmth of her clothes and car heater, even though she was sweating.

But there was something out there in the rain. Sandy could barely see it through the rain by looking into her rear view mirror. The peace she had previously felt disappeared and her heart raced as if it were trying to outrun her truck.

"How did he find me?!" exclaimed Sandy. "Surely, even a robot would have trouble finding me in this weather, especially with my phone dead. Does nothing slow down or stop this robot?"

But there was Pastor Matthew Love running behind her vehicle not more than a mile away. Sandy could not go any faster. Somehow she needed to find another way to ditch the robot.

At a fork, Sandy turned left and then at another left again. She was now once again on the usually busy street that she had been previously. Then to ensure that she would throw the robot off she drove across the double line that separated the two lanes of traffic going the same direction, and then turned around into a lane heading the opposite direction. Then she crossed another double line into another lane. Sandy stared into her rear view mirror. She no longer saw the shape of Pastor Matthew Love behind her. But as she was about to turn off onto another road, a loud siren blared behind her.

"Oh no!" shouted Sandy. "I didn't want the police involved in this. And I certainly don't need a ticket."

But she knew it would be no good trying to get away from the police, so obediently she pulled off to the side of the road and parked, waiting with anxiety. Behind her, not one, but two officers got out of the police car.

As the duo of officers approached Sandy's truck, she took out her wallet. Whatever the officers were about to say, Sandy suspected it would not be good, especially since they would have to talk to her whilst standing in the pouring rain. Neither of them were carrying an umbrella. Thus, Sandy was surprised that when the officers came to the window one was actually smiling. Although, his smile seemed familiar to her, even though she was sure she had never seen this officer before.

Both of the police officers were over six feet tall and dressed in standard police attire. The one not smiling seemed the older of the two, and he stared down sternly at Sandy through her window. Sandy quickly rolled down her window.

"May I see your driver's license, ma'am?" said the stern officer.

Sandy handed the officer her driver's license.

The police officer took it and looked at it.

"So, Sandy Schaffer," he said, looking up at Sandy once again just as sternly as before. "Why are you out on a night like this? Where are you headed?"

"To my sister's residence in another state."

"But why were you pulling those illegal maneuvers? Just because the road is empty doesn't mean you can just ignore the rules of the road."

Sandy hesitated. She knew her story would seem far-fetched, but she also knew she had no chance of stopping Pastor Matthew Love without help.

"I'm being pursued by a robot. The majority of my church's board, myself included, voted to make an Actually Authentic Android our pastor. We programmed the robot to the liking of the congregation, but now apparently it is going on a rampage. It's already killed one member of our board, Mark Stamos, and now I'm sure it means to kill me."

Almost abruptly, the stern look on the police officer's face vanished and he began to laugh.

"An Actually Authentic Android? Don't pull my leg," he said, gaining back some of his sternness.

"But it's true," protested Sandy. "Haven't you seen the ads? They look so much like a real human that you can't tell the difference and they're nearly indestructible. He was running in this ice storm without any problems, chasing my vehicle, and I had to pull those illegal maneuvers to get away from him."

Again, the officer laughed.

"Will you listen to this lady talk? She's nuts."

"Of course, she is," replied the other officer. "That ad about the Actually Authentic Android is just exaggerating. They do that frequently in ads. No robot could be that realistic looking and so indestructible."

As he continued to smile cheerfully, suddenly Sandy realized why his smile was so familiar.

"Why you're a robot too," she slowly intoned.

"What? Me a robot?" answered the smiling officer. "Of course, I'm not a robot. I'm Officer Mack McFinlay."

The once stern officer did not laugh this time, but instead rolled his eyes. Then he took out a pen and a pad and wrote on the pad.

"I'm issuing you a ticket for those illegal maneuvers."

He handed the ticket to Sandy. She took the ticket, and waited for the officers to dismiss her. Then something caught her attention. In the bushes some feet away, she caught sight of Pastor Matthew Love. She thought he was staring at her, but it was tough to tell when the only light came from the police car. The moon and the stars were hidden from view by the phantom clouds in the sky.

"It's Pastor Matthew Love," Sandy breathed. "He's still following me."

"What's that?" asked the officer, resuming his usual stern manner.

"It's the robot pastor. He's out to get me," Sandy shrieked, pointing to the bushes.

The stern officer again rolled his eyes. The other officer walked over quietly to the bushes, carefully checked in and around them, and then came back.

"There's nobody in the bushes, lady," he said, sounding very logical.

The stern officer looked very angry.

Stop trying to pull our leg, lady! If you don't stop it, we'll haul you in, and have your head examined. Now get out of here and make sure you don't break the law again."

Then he turned to the other officer.

"Come on, Mack. Let's get out of this damn rain."

Then with an angry huff he walked back to the patrol car, followed by Mack. They got into the vehicle and slowly drove off down the road. Sandy waited until they were out of sight before she started up her own vehicle. Before she drove off, she glanced again at the bushes. She did not see Pastor Matthew Love, but then again it was dark, almost as much as any basement with the lights out.

Sandy wanted to speed away, but she did not dare. If she went too fast she knew that she would spin out and crash into something. Frequently, as she drove she peered into her rear view mirror. Again, Sandy turned onto a side road. She drove a couple of blocks, then turned left. She went down another side street. This did not appear to be a nice neighborhood. Trash littered the sidewalks and the street. All the houses looked old, deteriorated, and dilapidated. Sandy went another two blocks and turned. She went another two blocks and turned. She turned again to the left after one block and after traveling another five blocks she turned right. She now had no idea where she was, but she hoped to God she had lost that robot.

Chapter 11

A Fortunate Accident

THE OLDEST AND LARGEST tree in town stood in an old cul-de-sac in an upper middle class neighborhood. It wasn't far away from where Sandy lived, but it was just a hair nicer than her neighborhood, and Sandy had never been down this particular street. Every window was dark as Sandy came to the cul-de-sac and every car properly stored away in the garage.

In the middle of the cul-de-sac in the soil in front of the sidewalk in front of the best and nicest of all the homes in the cul-de-sac stood the tree, its long branches reaching up left, right, front, and back like a giant squid. Down beside its gigantic trunk mounds of colorful leaves lay. Very few leaves remained on the tree's branches. The nearly naked monster was complete with a pair of holes in its trunk that gave it the impression of having eyes. The ice which had formed on many of its branches only added to its ghastly appearance.

Sandy did not like its looks when she drove up, even less so when she realized she was in a cul-de-sac. She stopped her truck, rolled down her window, and peered out. No drops of water descended on her head, but that was of little comfort to her.

"Great. A cul-de-sac. How on earth did I end up here?" Sandy sighed.

"Although this neighborhood isn't far from my house. I guess the robot wouldn't expect me to head back home. He's probably out on the highway looking for me."

"Now that wouldn't be logical, would it? Especially, when you're right here," came a calm voice.

Sandy's heart raced as Pastor Matthew Love came out from behind the beast of a tree, standing to the right of it and gazing at her.

"Well, Sandy you're being most illogical, don't you think?" went on the robot. "Why do you keep running from me? You know I'll eventually get you. And after all, you want to meet Jesus, don't you Sandy?"

Sandy abruptly exited her vehicle and stood tall, holding her loaded rifle, which she pointed dangerously at Pastor Matthew Love.

"What are you talking about, robot?" said Sandy, sarcastically. "I've already met Jesus. Somehow I doubt you ever will."

The robot didn't move, but only continued to look at her. She, however, took a step forward, still pointing her rifle at him. She had no face protection on and her nose tingled with cold. But at least it had stopped raining.

"Now what are you doing with that rifle, Sandy? You know you can't shoot me. The bullet will only bounce back and kill you. Come on. Drop the rifle. You've already lost."

Sandy said nothing further, but raising her rifle, fired fast shots in a row. The robot did not move. Cracks of ice broke upwards. Then more cracks clattered and branches plummeted toward the pastor until he was covered. Sandy stared at the pile of branches. None of them moved. Pastor Matthew Love made no noise, but at the sound of shots, angry and frightened shouts began to ascend from the houses in the cul-de-sac. Laughing, Sandy threw down her bulletless gun, entered her vehicle, put on her seatbelt, turned the key, and slowly and carefully turned her vehicle around in order to leave the cul-de-sac.

But no sooner had she put her foot to the gas when she heard more cracks of ice behind her. In her rear view mirror Sandy saw Pastor Matthew Love hurl ice encrusted branches off of him and into the air wildly. Sandy wanted to floor the gas pedal, but she dared not do so on an icy road even as a branch belted into her back window, flinging bits of glass toward her head. Sandy had just turned onto another street when Pastor Matthew Love again began running after her.

"What am I gonna do now?" asked Sandy inwardly. "This robot sure doesn't want to die. And he certainly doesn't want to give up. Looks like I'm gonna have to take more drastic measures to ditch him."

It was after midnight now and Sandy was getting sleepy. She usually went to bed at ten, if even that. Sandy fought to keep herself awake. She turned on the radio and a song from the 1960s blared through her speakers. This perked Sandy up, but not as much as the panic of seeing once again the robot in her rear view mirror, gaining on her.

There seemed to be nothing to do except continue on and finally, Sandy turned onto a main highway. The robot eased his pace and hid behind some bushes, still trying to follow her while concealing himself. Twenty minutes passed and not a single other vehicle came into view. Sandy had not seen the robot in the rear view mirror for a while when she approached an area of the road where there was a vicious drop to the right. She slowed down. She dared not hope that the railing would keep her truck from going over it.

Then she saw him again. Pastor Matthew Love was running after her faster and smoother than any race horse, showing no signs that the ice was any obstacle. Sandy again panicked.

"What do I do now?" she said, exasperated. "I can't go any faster here, especially on the ice."

She peered back at the robot who had almost reached her vehicle.

"Or can I?" she said, a devious look appearing on her face.

Removing one hand from the steering wheel, Sandy unbuckled her seatbelt. Pastor Matthew Love grabbed ahold of her vehicle and hoisted himself on top of it, seeming in no way to be in danger of falling off. Sandy unlocked the doors of her vehicle and floored the gas pedal. Immediately, Sandy's vehicle slid recklessly. Pastor Matthew Love, nevertheless, did not find himself thrown from the truck's roof. Sandy opened the drivers' side door and dove out. The vehicle carelessly plunged off the cliff with the pastor on it and into the deep ocean waters below.

Sandy stood up slowly on the icy road, sore with bruises from the impact of the dive. But despite the cold, her pain, and the loss of her rather nice vehicle, Sandy laughed.

"Take that Pastor Matthew Love!" she shouted.

Then she shivered and looked around at the dark, cold, icy world about her. It was not raining, but the wind blew fiercely, stinging her face.

"Oh dear," she said to herself. "Looks like I'm going to have quite a walk in the cold. But at least I've finally seen the last of that robot."

Chapter 12

Bob Says His Peace

Sandy walked around in the rain, which had started to fall not ten minutes after she had begun her journey. Her shoes were fortunately waterproof and so was her huge coat. Sandy had left her gloves in the truck and instead of letting her arms swing in a carefree fashion from side to side, they stood still, buried within the caverns of her very large pockets. Her scarf also had been left behind and met the same end as Sandy's sturdy truck. She had no hat either, but the heavy hood of her coat covered her head.

She had no idea where to go, but at least she knew where she was. She had traveled this road numerous times. If she followed it she would eventually come downtown where city hall, the fire department, the police station, and many nice restaurants and stores lay. But they were still almost ten miles away, and it would take her some time to get there without a vehicle.

But much worse than the length of the walk before her and even the rain that pelted her and the cold and the wind was the soreness of her legs that resulted from the perilous roll from her vehicle. While she was able to walk off some of the pain, it did not all dissipate. This, on top of her tiredness, slowed her down.

She wished she could lie down. If only she could find a motel. She wouldn't mind it in the least if there was no power as long as her room was clean and had a bed.

She had gone about two miles when she was finally greeted to the right by another road. This was not any wide highway or asphalt road of any kind, but rather a narrow road of dirt barely big enough that an average-sized car could be driven on it.

Sandy turned onto this road, and with some difficulty increased her walking speed. She immediately recognized this road and she knew one particular person who lived on it.

After another half mile Sandy approached a shabby-looking house on her left with a mailbox that read Wet. This was the home of Ernie Wet, the old fisherman who had been coming to her church for over twenty years.

There was nothing which Sandy hated more thoroughly than fish, yet somehow she always managed to find herself at Ernie Wet's house. She could not be more annoyed. All fish aside, Ernie Wet's house could not be uglier, and Ernie Wet himself any more irritating. He was always telling tedious, long stories and worn out, stupid jokes. The man could just never shut up.

But Sandy felt she had no choice but to endure Ernie today. She was wet, cold, and tired. At least she could sit on Ernie's old, brown couch for a while and then perhaps he would drive her home.

But to her horror, when she came closer to the door, Sandy found that it was no longer on its hinges, but lay in pieces inside the house's entrance. Sandy was startled. She looked around at her surroundings as if expecting to see someone staring back at her from some unknown hiding place. No eyes looked back at her.

Sandy turned her attention once again to the broken door. She was sure of one thing. This had not been done by the weather.

It was entirely dark inside Ernie Wet's house. Sandy shuddered. For a moment she did not dare move.

The rain became harder. She still hesitated for a moment. Then she entered.

She did have a flashlight on her, but again she hesitated to bring it out. It wasn't too long until she walked into a long, short table and almost tripped. Slowly, Sandy brought out her flashlight and turned it on.

She was in Ernie Wet's living room and she did not see Ernie Wet anywhere. But there was a half-eaten bowl of popcorn sitting on the coffee table, the very table she had run into.

"Ernie Wet! Ernie!" Sandy shouted.

There was no response. Sandy went to the staircase leading up to one of the bedrooms, the game room, and the second bathroom, and looked up it. But she did not go up.

"Maybe he is still asleep," she said to herself, although she somehow really doubted this. The broken door kept her mind at unease.

Cautiously, she crept into the kitchen. The refrigerator made no hum. The power had still not come back on. There was a white tile floor on the kitchen and when Sandy moved her red flashlight across the floor there was no mistaking what she saw dark splotches of on it. Sandy shuddered.

"It's blood. Dear God, what's happened here?"

She was afraid to look around any further. Tired as she was she headed back toward the front door, preparing once again to go trotting along in the cold rain. But when she came to the front door a new sight greeted her even more terrifying than what she had found in the kitchen. Ernie lay on the ground in a strange position, not moving. His eyes stared straight at her, but Sandy could tell there was nothing behind them. Despite her alarm, Sandy could not help to utter what came to her mind at that moment.

"Now at last has Ernie Wet shut up."

"Yes. He has," came a familiar monotone voice. "And so shall you."

Then to her utter shock and fright, Sandy saw Pastor Matthew Love standing in the doorway.

Sandy wanted to ask the android how it survived, but she did not dare hesitate. Immediately, she ran. The bedroom on the ground floor of Ernie's place had a sliding glass door. Sandy hoped to make her way through it and out the backyard gate, into the forest behind the house.

She had turned off her red flashlight as soon as she had beheld Pastor Matthew Love, and as soon as she was sure she had gotten out of his range of vision she noiselessly got down on the ground, crawling across the floor.

Pastor Matthew Love no longer had his lantern. It like Sandy's truck had been lost to the ocean. The robot fumbled to find the flashlight that was part of his person, but he could not find it.

"When I get back to the church I must find my owner's manual and read it," he said in the same monotone voice as before.

Meanwhile Sandy had made it into the bedroom with the sliding glass door. Quietly, she unlatched the door and slid it open. Then she crept under the bed, making use of the weird and elaborate collection of junk she found there to conceal herself from view. It was very dusty underneath the bed and it was with acute difficulty that Sandy kept from sneezing. There was also an odor which made Sandy want to gag, but she kept her reflex in check. She did not want to think about what might be under Ernie Wet's bed either.

Pastor Matthew Love entered the bedroom from the hallway. Sandy did all she could to remain silent. She didn't have much hope that her ruse would work. But she hoped that since leaving the house would appear more logical to the robot than hiding under the bed that the robot wouldn't even bother to look under there.

Pastor Matthew Love looked all around the room and then at the open sliding glass door. Without a word he walked over to the door and stepped outside. Sandy did not dare try to peek at him. She attentively listened to his movements. It was now not raining. Sunrise was only about three hours away, and while neither Sandy nor even the Actually Authentic Android knew it, the fierce ice storm would soon stop and again the bright sun would shine unhindered over the Fall landscape.

Pastor Matthew Love looked over toward the horizon where the sun would eventually appear. It was ways beyond Ernie Wet's backyard fence. Emotionlessly, the Actually Authentic Android scanned the backyard for some sign of Sandy, but he did not see one. He began to walk around to the other side of the house where the gate was, out of the view of the clear bedroom door.

Sandy heard his steps and then there was silence except for the sound of the wind as it blew through the trees, knocking off leaves and of the rain as it poured upon the world below. Sandy considered quitting her hiding place, but she waited to see first if the pastor had really gone. But Sandy's compulsion to sneeze finally caught up with her. The noise rattled in the room threateningly. Sandy almost gasped in response, but checked herself. For a moment it was quiet, but then came footsteps, and soon Pastor Matthew Love was back in the room.

"Yes. You are in here, aren't you?" he said, hypnotically. "Where are you hiding Sandy?"

Sandy lay as still as she could and pinched her nose shut.

"Now you don't have to fear me, Sandy," said the Actually Authentic Android. "After all, I'm Pastor Matthew Love and I'm here to tell you that Jesus loves you."

He ceased speaking for a moment and listened. His eyes gazed at the closed closet with sliding mirror doors, and then they burned toward the bed. Without another spoken word, the robot suddenly started singing an old hymn, which began with the words:

When peace like a river attendth my way
When sorrows like sea billows roll
Whatever my lot, Thou hast taught me to say
It is well, it is well with my soul[1]

Even in his emotionless, monotone voice, the hymn sounded truly beautiful. Even Sandy would have thought so had she not been filled with terror at the creature singing it. Before the last chorus of the hymn, Pastor Matthew Love halted. This terrified Sandy all the more. She knew she could not hope to sneak away from the pastor now. Her only chance was if he left.

Pastor Matthew Love did not look at the bed, but he gazed at the open door that led to the rest of the house.

---

1. Bliss and Spafford, *When Peace Like a River.*

"It is well with your soul now, isn't, Sandy?" asked the android, methodically.

Sandy did not answer. Suddenly the bed flung violently into the air, smashing into the wall. Sandy screamed and stood up. The robot eyed her indifferently. Sandy stared at the open door and then at the gun in Pastor Matthew Love's hand.

"The robot police officer gave you that, didn't he?" she asked, helplessly.

"Indeed, he did," answered the robot, remorselessly.

Sandy bolted for the door, but the robot blocked her. Then he grabbed her by the throat and lifted her from the ground. Sandy fought frantically and uselessly to get away. Pastor Matthew Love squeezed her throat and in the same emotionless, monotone voice he sang while looking in her eyes:

"It is well with your soul
It is well, it is well with your soul"

Then suddenly Sandy went limp and moved no more.

◆ ◆ ◆

It was about 4 a.m. and Sarah had awoken from her sleep. With the power having gone out, she and her husband had gone to bed. Usually, she was woken up by her alarm clock every morning, but this morning her body's clock woke her. She peered into the darkness at her husband who lay beside her, snoring as loudly as a freight train.

"My Bob makes more noise asleep than awake," she thought, amazed.

She glanced to the right of her at her alarm clock, which blinked red numbers over and over again, signaling to her that she needed to reset the time on it. Sarah sat up and switched on the lamp, which sat on the same little table as her alarm clock. The light hurt Sarah's eyes for a moment, but it did nothing to stir Bob.

"Wake up, Bob!" Sarah shouted. "It's time to milk the cow."

Sarah leaned over and elbowed her husband, but Bob did not budge. Then she shook him and finally opening his eyes, he turned over and looked at her. Bob sat up in the bed, but remained silent. Sarah leaned over, put her arm around him, and kissed his cheek.

"How did you sleep, my love?" Sarah asked tenderly.

In response, Bob reached over to the table next to his side of the bed and grabbed a handful of jelly beans from a bowl and stuffed them into his mouth. Sarah laughed good-naturedly and then hugged Bob hard so that he nearly swallowed the jelly beans. Then she got up off the bed and got dressed. Then she trotted off to the kitchen to make breakfast. Meanwhile, Bob had barely gotten himself up off the bed.

◆ ◆ ◆

It was still dark and fairly cold when Bob finally made it outside to go to the barn to feed and milk their only cow. She was quite an ugly cow, but gentle as long as no one touched her udders with cold hands. Bob's hands were warm in his mittens and he hated having to take the mittens off even in the barn. But as he approached the cow, Bob heard a sound behind him and turned around. Then out of the shadows stepped Pastor Matthew Love holding Mack's gun, which was pointed straight at Bob.

"Hello Bob," said the android.

"Oh crap," squeaked Bob, and with a bang from the gun he collapsed onto the floor of the barn.

Chapter 13

The End?

"THESE EVENTS ARE TRULY as baffling as they are disturbing," said Police Chief Jackson to Detective Mallard who was typing notes into his tablet quickly. "I don't have any leads. I had a talk with Pastor Matthew Love this morning. He had heard about it all on the news and did not know why it had happened. He had just finished some coffee and cookies when the power went out. So, he went to sleep until morning. Then he got up and turned on the television and there it all was. I certainly don't suspect he had anything to do with these deaths and disappearances."

Detective Mallard nodded.

"I agree. You said he was voted in by the church board and the whole congregation declared him their pastor after he preached his first sermon. I don't sense any animosity between him and the congregation at all."

"Nope," said the police chief, grinning slightly. "He seems like a darn good fellow."

"Yes. We can forget him as a suspect. Now one of the known deaths may have been just an accident. Hubert died in a fire started by a lit joint and probably being careless with his lighter. The only reason I have to suspect that foul play might have been involved is because several church board members were murdered. Mark was stabbed twice by two different knives. Bob and Mary were shot. Dottie was hanged from her own ceiling fan. Sandy was strangled. She was found at the home of another member of the church who was not a member of the church board named Ernie Wet. He was found on his living room floor stabbed through the chest. Two other board members, Madeline and Buford, are missing. I haven't the faintest clue where to start looking for them. Also, another member of the church who was not on the board, Amber, was found dead in her car just outside Mark's house. Her husband couldn't figure out why she would have been there nor did he have any idea who would want to kill her or anyone from their church."

Police Chief Jackson looked as bewildered as the detective.

"The only board member who was seen after the board meeting that afternoon was Sandy. Two comrades of mine stopped her for illegal driving maneuvers and issued her a ticket. Whatever was she doing out in a bad storm like that? Though my comrades mentioned that she said she was headed out of state. That in itself is a kind of clue."

"Indeed," answered Detective Mallard, appearing deep in thought. "Likely, someone didn't like these board members and these two others too much. Maybe the missing ones simply skipped town. I'll find out."

He started walking towards the steps to get inside the church. Then he paused briefly and turned to the police chief.

"Well, I don't normally do this, but I'm already here. You want to go to church too, Jackson?"

"Sure," said Police Chief Jackson, smiling enthusiastically. "I am eager to hear Pastor Matthew Love preach."

The two of them began walking up to the entrance of the church. The sun shown overhead brightly bathing the church steps with light.

"I'll get back to the case on Monday," answered the detective, resolutely. "I'll find this psycho serial killer who murdered all these people."

"You really think a serial killer is behind this?" inquired Police Chief Jackson.

"Of course," stated Detective Mallard, matter-of-factly. "Who but a serial killer would be mad enough to roam around in an ice storm murdering people?"

"Exactly," answered Police Chief Jackson. "No normal human being would do that."

Then without saying another word to one another they headed up into the church.

◆ ◆ ◆

Pastor Matthew Love stood in his pulpit surveying the crowd who had gathered this morning. All of them except for a few newcomers dressed up for the occasion: dresses, skirts, dress shirts, dress pants, ties, fancy, shiny shoes, tall heels, and floppy flats. Pastor Matthew Love himself wore a new suit this morning. He wore a spiffy dark blue suit with a white shirt and a plaid tie.

As time for the service to start came to pass, everyone in the sanctuary became silent and all eyes fixed upon Pastor Matthew Love. He did not smile, but with a look of seemingly earnest seriousness he began to speak to the people present.

"My brothers and sisters, they grieve me as they grieve our Lord these great tragedies that have befallen our community. Our congregation has lost some wonderful God-fearing folks, all of whom we can be sure are home in heaven with our Lord Jesus Christ. It is the unfortunate truth that none of us here knows the time or day or the circumstances of our death. But for all of us who have accepted Jesus Christ into our hearts we are assured that we will go to heaven when we die, that wonderful place where there is no pain, grief, or death.

There is nothing my brothers and sisters that anyone can do that can put them beyond the saving power of our Lord Jesus Christ. Even whoever is responsible for these horrible events can be forgiven for their sins if only they will ask Jesus Christ for forgiveness and ask him to come into their heart. While we might be tempted to hate this person, we must remember that our God wants us to forgive and love our enemies, to pray for them, and to treat them with kindness. Afterall, remember what an awful punishment would await them in hell. We should pity this person and hope for their redemption in Christ.

Also, let us remember today that God comforts all those who mourn. Our God even mourns with us. Remember how Jesus mourned at the tomb of his friend, Lazarus. We are not alone in this time of tragedy."

Many in the congregation, being overcome with grief, began to weep. Pastor Matthew Love closed his eyes, bowed his head, and began to pray:

"Heavenly Father, comfort us today. Forgive us and our enemies of sin. Let us know your love and share that love with the world. In Jesus's name, amen."

Then Pastor Matthew Love raised his head and opened his eyes. He waved his hand and bid the congregation to depart in peace. With many of the congregation still weeping, they all rose and began to leave.

But two in the crowd tarried. These did not weep, but they came forward with enthusiasm. Pastor Matthew Love began to walk toward them. Approaching, one of them greeted the pastor and shook hands with him. Then he introduced the man with him. Pastor Matthew Love shook hands with this man and said:

"Hello. I'm Pastor Matthew Love and I'm here to tell you that Jesus loves you."

Then on Pastor Matthew Love's face formed the most pleasant and charming smile anyone could possibly imagine.

The End!!!

www.ingramcontent.com/pod-product-compliance
Lightning Source LLC
Chambersburg PA
CBHW071346130626
46556CB00005B/2059